W9-BJH-870

Tyrannosaurus Math

by Michelle Markel

Illustrated by Doug Cushman

SCHOLASTIC INC.

New York Toronto London Auckland
Sydney Mexico City New Delhi Hong Kong

A colossal THANK YOU to Pete Makovicky, PhD, Associate Curator of Dinosaurs, Department of Geology, Field Museum, Chicago; Luis Chiappe, PhD, Curator and Director, The Dinosaur Institute of the Natural History Museum of Los Angeles County; Timothy J. Kessler, Elementary Math Advisor, Los Angeles Unified School District; and Daniele Della Gala, National Board Certified Teacher, Los Angeles Unified School District. —M. M.

No part of this publication may be reproduced, stored in a retrieval system, or transmitted in any form or by any means, electronic, mechanical, photocopying, recording, or otherwise, without written permission of the publisher. For information regarding permission, write to Tricycle Press, an imprint of Random House Children's Books, a division of Random House, Inc., 1745 Broadway, New York, NY 10019.

ISBN 978-0-545-30233-3

Text copyright © 2009 by Michelle Markel. Illustrations copyright © 2009 by Doug Cushman. All rights reserved. Published by Scholastic Inc., 557 Broadway, New York, NY 10012, by arrangement with Tricycle Press, an imprint of Random House Children's Books, a division of Random House, Inc. SCHOLASTIC and associated logos are trademarks and/or registered trademarks of Scholastic Inc.

12 11 10 9 8 7 6 5 4 3 2 1   10 11 12 13 14 15/0

Printed in the U.S.A.   08

First Scholastic printing, October 2010

Design by Katie Jennings
Typeset in Black Beard
The illustrations in this book were rendered in acrylic.

To Dad, for his wild stories
—M. M.

For Rudy
—D. C.

PRONUNCIATION GUIDE

Ankylosaur: AN-kuh-loh-sore
Hadrosaur: HA-druh-sore
Ornithomimus: orn-ITH-oh-MY-mus
Triceratops: try-SER-uh-tops
Tyrannosaurus: tuh-rah-nuh-SORE-us

One muggy morning, a dinosaur burst from his shell.

"My, what big claws I have!" he marveled, as he counted his fingers. "And what big toes I've got!" He counted those too. Then he added his fingers and toes together, making a number sentence.

"Go figure!" his mother cried, and she named him Tyrannosaurus Math.

$$4 + 6 = 10$$

Crack! Crack! Out popped two tyrannosaurus brothers.
Crack! Crack! Crack! Out popped three tyrannosaurus sisters.
"Hmm, that's me, plus two, plus three," he thought, and
reckoned how many kids were in his family.

2

4

6

8

10

By the time he was one, T-Math could count by twos.
He counted all the footprints of the ornithomimus
until they disappeared near the river.

T-Math learned his fives. He learned his tens.
Even before he was old enough to eat them,
he counted a whole herd of triceratops.

5

10

15

20

T-Math became a huge show-off around his family.
One afternoon he gobbled up 263 dragonflies, and his
brother gobbled up 259.

"Guess who ate the greater number?" he asked.

"Oh, what's the difference?" his brother exclaimed.
T-Math knew that, too.

And he checked his answer by adding, just to be sure.

$$\begin{array}{r} 2\overset{5}{\cancel{6}}\overset{1}{3} \\ -\ 259 \\ \hline 4 \end{array} \qquad \begin{array}{r} \overset{1}{2}59 \\ +\ \ \ 4 \\ \hline 263 \end{array}$$

Soon T-Math could get his mouth around small herbivores. One day he devoured thirty-nine pounds of meat, and a few days later, he scarfed down sixty-two more pounds.

"Ma!" he yelled. "How much do you think I've eaten lately?"

"Enough to make you a colossal genius," his mother said.

$$\begin{array}{r} {}^{1}39 \\ + 62 \\ \hline 101 \end{array}$$

As the tyrant lizard grew and grew, his math skills became greater and greater.

At his full size, nothing was scarier than the sight of T-Math thundering through the forest, chewing on a problem in his head.

His mind was as sharp as his teeth, and he totaled them every chance he got.

"I got a good one!" he announced one day during lunch. "If I ate three ankylosaurs, with four tasty legs each, how many legs would I eat in all?"

"We give up," his sister groaned. "How many?"

T-Math picked up a stick. "Try drawing a picture!"

$3 \times 4 = 12$

It seemed like nothing could stop that bone-munching, number-crunching Tyrannosaurus Math. When a hurricane struck, he made a pictograph of the leaves torn from the trees.

When a meteorite sped toward the earth, he asked himself, "sphere or cube?" before dashing for safety.

And when a volcano launched colorful rocks onto the plain, he arranged them in rows to count them swiftly before the lava caught up to him.

Then, one afternoon as T-Math went hunting with his brother and sister, they spotted six hadrosaurs out for a stroll.

"Dibs on the three big ones," said T-Math's brother.

"That's not fair!" snapped his sister.

"Wait!" T-Math said. "We can share them equally. Know how many we'd each get?"

"Oh, who cares?" his sister said, stomping away.

T-math called after her, "We can each have a big one *and* a small one! Two out of six total . . . that's one-third for each of us!"

At that moment the earth began to shake. Then it began to rumble. Trees toppled. Boulders tumbled. The ground split open! T-Math and his brother heard a cry.

"Help!"

They found themselves on one side of a deep canyon, while their terrified sister stood on the other.

For the first time in his life, T-Math didn't know what to do. He twiddled his claws. He squinted. He thrashed his tail to and fro. Then he asked himself, "How far across is the gap?" He looked down at his feet. Around twenty of those, he estimated.

T-Math counted his footsteps as he walked alongside a
fallen tree. "Let's swing this trunk across the gulch,"
he said to his brother. Together, they made a bridge
for their sister and she quickly clambered to safety.

"Who knew math could be so useful?" she said.

"You'll have to teach us more of your tricks," said his brother.

From that day on, it seemed there was no problem that the megalizard and his family couldn't solve.

Well, *almost*. One evening, they tried to count the stars. T-Math's brother counted to fifty. His sister counted to one hundred. T-Math counted to one thousand, but there were too many little sparkles, scattered across an endless sky. His eyes were getting bleary. "There could be a billion stars up there," he sighed.

"Good use of estimation!" his mom exclaimed.
"Group hug!" the kids all roared.
And they all lived mathematically ever after.

$E = mc^2$

$v = \dfrac{dx}{dt}$

Tyrannosaurus Math Skills

Addition: T-Math adds his fingers and toes to find out the total. Then he uses addition to count his newly-hatched siblings. Later he adds together all the pounds of meat he has eaten. *pp. 5, 7, 13*

Number sentence: Using math symbols (+ and =), T-Math makes equations. *pp. 5, 7*

Skip counting: T-Math counts the footprints of the ornithomimus in multiples of two. Later, he counts a herd of triceratops by grouping them in multiples of five. *pp. 8-9, 10-11*

Ordering and comparing whole numbers: T-Math determines whether he or his brother ate the greater number of dragonflies. *p. 12*

Subtraction: Using subtraction, T-Math finds the difference between the number of dragonflies that he and his brother ate. *p. 12*

Inverse relationships/operations: To check his subtraction, T-Math uses addition. *p. 12*

Symmetry: T-Math notices that the right and left sides of his mouth contain the same number and type of teeth. *p. 15*

Multiplication: Applying his understanding of symmetry, T-Math multiplies the number of teeth on one side of his mouth by two to get the total number of teeth. *pp. 15, 17*

Reasoning: T-Math shows that a math problem can be solved by sketching a picture. To represent the multiplication of 3 x 4, he draws three ankylosaurs with four legs each. *p. 17*

Organizing data with graphs: T-Math makes a pictograph to organize and compare the number of different leaves he finds after a hurricane. *p. 19*

Geometric shapes: By comparing a meteorite to solid geometric shapes, T-Math demonstrates his understanding of their differences. *p. 20*

Arrays: T-Math arranges colorful rocks in columns and rows that are easy to multiply. *p. 21*

Division and Fractions: To show that he, his sister, and brother can each get an equal share of 6 hadrosaurs, T-Math divides the number of hadrosaurs by 3 and names the fraction of the set. *p. 23*

Nonstandard measurement: To find out the length of a fallen tree, T-Math uses his foot as a unit of measurement. *pp. 26-27*

Estimation: Up for any math challenge, T-Math makes an approximate calculation of the number of stars in the sky. *(Note: T-Math couldn't possibly see all the stars in the universe. Scientists estimate that there are billions and billions of them!) pp. 28-29*